Don't F[...] to Chew Your Food!

Get Chrissy

ISBN: 978-1-949265-00-2 (Paperback)
ISBN: 978-1-949265-01-9 (Ebook)

Library of Congress Control Number: 2019906587

This is a work of fiction. Names, characters, businesses, places, events, locales, and incidents are either the products of the author's imagination or used in a fictitious manner. Any resemblance to actual persons, living or dead, or actual events is purely coincidental.

Front Cover image by Shon Watkins

First printing edition 2019.

GetChrissy
P.O. Box 582
Gardena, CA 90248

www.getchrissy.com

CHAPTER ONE

The Corridor of Hues

MANNY AND BROOKS were full of excitement while sharing the news of their discovery with their sister, Jewels. The two brothers loved to go out on adventures to discover new places to explore.

Their village was very old, and Brooks and Manny always tended to come across something that would attract their attention, whether it was a broken object that had been thrown away, or an unusual creature that lurked around the shadows of the village.

"Jewels, you have to come take a look at this place with us," Manny said. "It's beautiful and mystical. I really believe we're on to something!"

Jewels was sitting on her favorite lounge chair, knitting. "On to what?"

Jewels thought everyone else in the village was ordinary and routine, but not Manny and Brooks. Those two could not sit still for one moment. If they weren't looking for some place to explore, they were putting together their next invention. Something always found a way to keep the wheels in those brains of theirs spinning.

"What's wrong with you guys?" Jewels said. "Do you know what they call you two around here?"

"Not really, and I don't care," Brooks said.

"Well, you should care!" Jewels said. "You two are getting the label of troublemakers in this village."

"Troublemakers?" Manny laughed. "Are you kidding me? The people in this village are lifeless and dull. I can barely stay awake around here!"

"It doesn't matter," Jewels said. "Getting labeled like this is not a good look for us as a family."

"Well, that's just too bad!" Manny said. "That's just how the ball bounces. Everyone can't be cut from the same cookie cutter. We are all different, despite what the people in this village may believe!"

"Right!" Brooks walked to a chair to sit alongside Manny. "Everyone else should learn that there are places beyond this village. A new exciting world yet to be discovered!"

"You two are hopeless!" Jewels sighed.

"So, do you want to hear about our little adventure? Or not?" Manny asked.

"Sure. I'm going to hear about it sooner or later," Jewels said.

"We discovered a small village, hidden in the far east of the forest," Manny said.

"Yup!" Brooks said. "It's like a whole new world there. It's so different from this place. You have to come with us next time!"

"Yes, Jewels," Manny said. "You have to come with us. We believe we may have found the village within the pages of the Corridor of Hues."

Jewels stood from her lounge chair and walked over to her brothers.

The Corridor of Hues were books that held the most beautiful oil paintings and portraits. However, the paintings were of the brightest shades of colors that were foreign to the village. These strange, unusual colors strayed from their typical, colorless world. The Corridor of Hues led the village to believe these bright, mysterious colors were wicked, bringing the curse of Locky disease upon the village. Throughout the centuries, these books had mysteriously trickled their way into the village.

Just the thought of Locky made Jewels shiver. When the victims were found, their tongues would be a very bright color. The disease made its victims very weak. Their hearing would fail, and vision would fade. Soon enough, they couldn't speak, and their bodies would tremble as they slowly drifted away.

Those who were caught with one of the books from the Corridor of Hues were removed from the village, along with the other criminals who were cast out. Rarely was a lawbreaker able to return to the village. They were often found in a diseased state and unable to tell their experience outside of the village, which made it a great mystery amongst the villagers indeed.

Even so, many villagers did not believe in the story of the Corridor of Hues. These were usually the troublemakers and lawbreakers. They explained that the

villagers that had been done away with possibly moved to
an unknown village beyond the forest. Those who came
back with the horrible Locky disease had possibly caught
the illness through an infected animal or an insect that was
unknown to the villagers. Though, they could never explain
the mysterious bright color that painted the victims'
tongues.

"What in the world were you two doing, going past
the forest of the village?" Jewels asked.

"It's called adventure and fun. That's what we
were doing!" Manny stuck his tongue out at her.

"Did you see anyone there?"

"No one, which was very strange," Brooks said,
"but there was a weird smell coming from the village."

"Oh yes, I remember that smell. I thought that was
coming from you, Brooks!" Manny laughed.

"No, that smell was not coming from me," Brooks
said. "I know how to use soap and water, thank you."

* * * * *

As the two brothers discussed their journey to the
mystical village, Jewels thought about their discovery.
Could it be? Had they found the village inside the Corridor

of Hues? Was there such a place where those rich and delightful colors blossomed?

Their village was lifeless and dull, and she knew her brothers were right. Jewels was no different than her brothers. Though not an explorer or inventor like they were, she was fascinated with their adventures, and the Corridor of Hues.

Jewels, at an early age, discovered one of the books while passing through the village. She had already seen many that were burned near the furnaces of the village. Fortunately, she was able to rescue one that was missed from sight. She hid it for many years, and it was her only access to the bright, enchanted world.

Jewels had always been teased for her name. She was named after the brightest and most beautiful stones known in the world. The more she was teased for her name, the more her attraction grew for these enchanting colors, which led her to hide the book for so long.

Her brothers Manny and Brooks were mistreated as well. The village had become annoyed with the two brothers and spoke unpleasantly of them. Most of the villagers hated that they were uninterested in the way of life there. It was rumored that if they did not stop causing trouble, they would be removed from the village.

Jewels knew that her brothers were a couple of young lads full of curiosity and life, and the village could never do such a thing to them. There were, however, times when she wondered if the villagers were right. Maybe, she shouldn't defend behavior that could threaten her and her brothers to be thrown out with the lawbreakers. Though, this time seems different. This time, her brothers may have found something incredible!

Over the following weeks, Jewels often thought about her brothers' discovery. Oh, how lovely it would be for her to visit this mysterious village. She thought about what she would do first. Would she smell the stunning, bright flowers while gazing upon the dazzling, blue sky? What a wonderful discovery these two had come across!

One morning, while Jewels daydreamed about the colorful paradise, she heard a knock at the door.

"Coming!" Jewels said.

She looked out the window and saw it was Mayor Pipers. He was an old man but loved and respected by many. He was dressed in dark overalls, with a hat, and boots. She let him inside her small cottage and offered him a seat in the den.

"Hello, Mayor Pipers!" Jewels said. "What brings you to my neck of the woods?"

"Where are your brothers, Jewels?" Mayor Pipers asked.

"Oh goodness! Who even knows?" Jewels said. "They are probably figuring out how to grow trees that can make oatmeal for breakfast."

Mayor Pipers looked at her, then turned his attention to an open book on the night stand near her favorite lounge chair.

It was the Corridor of Hues.

"Where did you get that?" Mayor Pipers face twisted in rage. "We destroyed all of the Corridor of Hues throughout the village!"

Jewels stood motionless against the door. "I found it laying in the bushes near the village quarters, but I didn't realize it had bright colors. I will make sure that it's put in the furnace later."

Mayor Pipers stared at her. "The village wants your brothers gone."

Jewels looked at him without much surprise. "Oh? Manny and Brooks told me on many occasions they don't care what anyone thinks about their adventurous nature."

"Adventurous nature?" Mayor Pipers said. "Is that what they call being stupid these days?"

Jewels just looked at Mayor Pipers.

"There's also been rumors of you seen with the Corridor of Hues, and judging from what I have just witnessed, confirms the rumors beyond a shadow of a doubt!"

"Mayor Pipers, surely you would think more highly of me than this. After all, I've—"

Mayor Pipers threw his hand up to silence her. He walked over to her with the Corridor of Hues which had been left open. The mayor pointed to the top of the page. It showed Jewels handwriting from when she had first found the book, and it read, *my world, my dream, one day it will be, with hope. -Jewels.*

Jewels stood next to the door and felt her legs giving way. She grabbed the doorknob to keep herself from falling.

"You're no better than your brothers!" Mayor Pipers yelled.

"What did you just say to me?" Jewels said.

"Did you not hear me the first time?"

Jewel's legs soon felt better. She let go of the doorknob that had held up her body, scrunched her fist and looked him straight in the eye. "Oh, I heard what you said. I just can't believe you would say that to me. As much as I have done for this village, and the sacrifices that I have made!"

"You and your brothers don't fit in here. Especially your brothers!" Mayor Pipers threw her beloved book on the ground."

Jewels heart ached, looking at the book on the floor.

"Your brother's discoveries, strange inventions, and other monkeyshines are ridiculous. The virtue of this village rests in my hands and those two have to go!"

Jewels looked at him without saying a word.

"This hurts me more than you'll ever know," Mayor Pipers said. "You have been loyal to this village. That's why I'm disappointed that it has come to this. I have been doing my best to keep your brothers here. It's come to a point where I can only do so much with my power."

"How dare you come into my home and tell me these things!" Jewels yelled.

"Remember who you are speaking to, Jewels."

"I know exactly who I'm speaking to," Jewels said. "I'm speaking to someone who has forgotten about my service and loyalty to this village. If you hadn't, you wouldn't have the heart to say such things!"

"I cannot stop them from pushing your brothers out any longer. The village, and I, have voted them out." A tear fell from Mayor Pipers' face. "Jewels, since my wife's passing, I have been alone. I could make a way for you to stay, if you give me your hand as my wife."

Jewels looked at him, more horrified than surprised by his request. She watched the mayor and her eyes roamed him from head to toe. He was a tall man with long feet, who kept himself slender. He was well spoken, highly educated, and one of the most powerful men in the village. On the other hand, Mayor Pipers was more than twice her age, an aged man with a collection of wrinkles.

The mayor turned to leave from her home. Before turning the knob, he took a quick glance back to where the Corridor of Hues laid. It was still open and resting peacefully on the floor. He looked over at Jewels, who noticed the bright glow from the book.

"You make sure that thing gets thrown in the furnace," the old mayor said. "If you are ever found with it again, you will be removed from this village at once. Even if you are to be my wife!"

He then opened the door and left from her home.

CHAPTER TWO

Someone New

JEWELS RAN TO where the Corridor of Hues lay and picked the book up from the floor to place it on the night stand again. She was in a nightmare! Her mind raced, thinking of the mayor's request and then racing back to her dear brothers, Manny and Brooks.

Through their childhood, she often witnessed them creating inventions that would get them in heaps of trouble. Jewels would sneak behind their bedroom door as she watched them in amazement. Oh, how creative those two were! As her brothers grew into young men, she continued to be amazed with their talents.

She had secretly loved their adventurous nature, but never dared to admit this. Good heavens, she would have been branded the same as they were. Jewels wanted to stay under the radar and behave properly to what was expected of the village women.

Jewels knew she was attractive, and the village believed it was a shame for a maiden to be unmarried after a certain time. She knew this all too well but kept herself busy and of service to the village. Just the other day she was helping several families with their harvest. She made clothes for the poorer families and visited the elderly and sick. Due to her efforts, the villagers often overlooked this shortcoming.

Manny and Brooks were the only two young men in the village who were not married. When asked why they had not taken on wives they would always respond, "If we ever meet any ladies around here that would like to explore with us and figure out how to make a hat that can teleport around the village and could serve us breakfast in bed, then maybe we will consider it."

Their rebellious attitude did not agree with the way of life in the village. The two brothers had brought shame to their family, and this angered Jewels. She believed they couldn't even hide their unusual behaviors. Their pride had gotten too much in the way of that. They wanted the entire village to know how strange they were.

Jewels' secrets were hidden, or so she had thought. She never spoke a word to anyone about having one of the Corridor of Hues. Mayor Pipers had said she was rumored around the village with it.

What in the world was I thinking? Did I get lazy about my secret?

"I've been around my brothers too long. Their carelessness has finally rubbed off on me!" Jewels said.

To think of life without her brothers was unbearable. Her only flesh and blood would be taken away from the village was unthinkable. Their penalty grew heavy on her heart. The villagers despised them, but she never imagined this would happen so suddenly. She had to make plans to talk with them. She wanted to warn them, so they could get their acts together. Maybe, it wasn't too late.

Later that day, Jewels invited her brothers over to speak with them.

"He said what?" Manny's eyes grew so big with surprise that they seemed to be popping out of his head.

"You heard me. You guys are out of here!" Jewels said.

Brooks mouth dropped open. "The people in this village have lost their minds."

Jewels walked over toward them and then took a seat on her favorite lounge chair. "He asked for my hand."

"What is he supposed to do with your hand?" Manny said.

The two brothers laughed at her.

"You know what I mean." Jewels rolled her eyes. "He wants my hand in marriage."

Manny and Brooks looked at each other and almost vomited.

"Gross!" Manny said. "I hope you turned him down. Old man Pipers has grandkids older than we are!"

Brooks immediately walked across from the lounge chair where his sister was and sat down directly in front of her.

"We are being booted out of here for what?" Brooks said. "For being different? Because we don't operate like these people do? Or it is because we just know how to have a good time?"

"This is an outrage!" Manny looked at Jewels. "The mayor had the nerve to tell you this? I have been saying for years that old man Pipers should have retired as the mayor long ago. He's wanted us out of here since the beginning. This whole thing is solely his doing! What needs to happen to him is—"

"Don't worry about what needs to happen to him," Jewels said. "You need to worry about what's going to happen to you. Remember he is in power, not you!"

"So, what do we do now?" Brooks said.

"What you do is ask for forgiveness in front of the whole village," Jewels said. "You can explain to them that your shenanigans were just a phase you both were going through, and that you are ready to put these foolish behaviors behind you to become upstanding and loyal citizens."

"I guess we don't have a choice," Brooks said. "I guess that's it."

"Yes," Jewels said. "If you show them that you are sorry. I'm sure you two will be granted your forgiveness."

Manny sat there silently and said nothing. He sat still with a frightening stare while looking towards the ceiling, rocking back and forth.

Jewels watched him, feeling her body tensing up.

Manny leaped to his feet and paced around the den of the cottage. He paced from wall to wall with that same strange look, then stopped.

"Forget this place. I'm out of here!" Manny yelled.

"What?" Jewels said.

"Yes, you heard right," Manny said. "I'm out of here. I'm gone. Who needs this place? Not me, and not you either Brooks!"

"Excuse me?" Brooks said. "Where are we supposed to be going? As terrible as this place is, we can't survive without it."

Manny walked over to Brooks. "Do you not remember that wonderful village we discovered weeks ago? I truly believe we discovered where the Corridor of Hues came from. That place has got to be it! It's a paradise compared to this place!"

"Count me in!" Brooks smiled from ear to ear.

Neither Jewels nor Manny had seen him so happy before.

"Yes!" Manny said. "Let's start getting ready to get out of this place. They want us out of here so bad, then fine! I'm sure that other village will be more than happy to have us there."

Jewels gave Manny a firm stare. "You said you didn't see anyone there. So, who exactly is supposed to welcome you two?"

"Look, Jewels," Manny said. "I'm sure we didn't see anyone because they're probably like us. They are explorers and inventors who appreciate the adventure in life. They don't hide around their village all day like these folks here!"

Manny grabbed Brooks and hurried him toward the door.

"Brooks!" Jewels jumped from her seat. "Please don't listen to Manny. He's not in his right mind. You saw his mental state earlier. He needs to lie down and take rest."

Brooks freed himself from Manny's hold and walked back over to his sister, Jewels. "I'm not going to be a puppet around this village for anyone. I refuse to pretend to be something that I was never supposed to be. But guess what, Jewels? You're no better than we are!"

Jewels chuckled. "Excuse me? I'm nothing like you or Manny. I follow the rules around here."

Both brothers looked at each other and laughed—falling to the floor.

"What's so funny?" Jewels said.

"You!" Manny yelled. "You're a fraud. Just the simple fact that you have kept this act up all these years has been very impressive."

"What act?" Jewels put her hands on her hips.

Brooks and Manny picked themselves up from the floor, tripping over each other.

"Everything about you is a lie!" Brooks shouted. "We know that you have one of the Corridor of Hues and you've been hiding it for years."

"That's right, dear sister." Manny put a little smirk on his face. "The rumors of your little secret have now been exposed by Mayor Pipers when he was here earlier. We over heard his announcement. He told everyone in the village about your well-hidden secret."

"Although, it's been rumored you've been seen with the book as of late, anyhow," Brooks said. "Now, the villagers know for certain you are just like us!"

Jewels felt lost in the wake of their confession.

"So, you knew about the rumors of my little secret? Yet, the rumors about you two being kicked out of here seemed to have gone right over your heads!"

"Or maybe we were just in denial about it." Manny's voice became harsher. "The same way you are in denial about yourself."

Jewels cut her eyes at Manny.

"We saw how you secretly hid behind doors to watch us," Manny said. "Every now and then, we would hear you pull up a chair around our room hoping to hear about our next adventure, as you pretended to knit or sew. Over the years, you showed hate towards the things we have spoken of and done. You acted as if you're uninterested, but as your interest grows your face lights up. We eventually caught on to your phony disguise. You are not like them here and remember that!"

Manny stormed out and slammed the door behind him.

Brooks followed, but turned to look back at his sister, Jewels. "You have always tried to fit in here. You are our blood and the apple doesn't fall far from the tree. You've denied yourself for so very long, and this has grown a wedge between us. We never hid who we were even if our bravery meant we would be kicked out from this village. We always were true to ourselves."

Jewels, stung by his words, gazed down toward the floor.

"Jewels listen to me." Brooks opened the door to leave from the cottage. "I have to go see where Manny has run off to. Despite what he said, we can't just take off until we figure things out first. We both want you to come with us, but either way, we will return to say our goodbyes."

After Brooks said those words, he closed the door and left to find his brother.

* * * * *

Jewels sat in her lounge chair where she would gaze upon the lovely paintings inside the Corridor of Hues. She thought about what Brooks had said to her, and how her world had been changing before her eyes.

Her brothers were being forced out of the village, but she had a choice to stay. This choice meant she would be driven out with her brothers or marry a man whom she didn't love and rid herself of her beloved book, the very book she tried to hide from the world for so long.

Just the thought that she would part from the Corridor of Hues made start to cry. This must be how her brothers felt about their passion for what they love. They couldn't bear to part with that reality of having it stripped away.

Jewels grabbed the Corridor of Hues and flipped through the pages of the book. Happiness came into her heart while she looked at the beautiful, artistic portraits. Her sadness quickly faded away.

"Those colors are a sign. Manny and Brooks were right. I don't belong here!" Jewels said.

Jewels took a good look at herself in her full-length mirror, taking her attention to her dress. It was dark, old-fashioned, and just plain ugly. She had always believed the village's clothing to be awful.

The dresses for the women and girls were not suitable to wear unless they were past their ankles, sitting on the top of their feet. If their dresses were even an inch higher than what was acceptable, they would be labeled as a trollop. With time, trollops were also removed from the grounds of the village.

But oh, how she hated the hot days when the dresses would cause her to sweat so severely because of the thick material. She was sick of it. She wanted to feel the air on her arms and legs while basking in the warm breeze.

In an echo of the dress code, the women in the village were only allowed to wear their hair up in a tight knit bun and were never allowed to cut it. Wearing their hair down was forbidden and doing so would cause shame upon the woman and her family.

"All these rules around here!" Jewels reached for her cutters from inside the table drawer.

She cut her dress right below the knee and took the pins from out of her hair, using her scissors to hack away at her hair too. When she was finished, her hair sat cut right above her shoulders.

She looked in the mirror and this time she saw someone else, someone new, and a smile curled across her lips.

CHAPTER THREE

Voyage to Paradise

SHE HEARD A noise near her home and glanced out
the window. Outside, Brooks walked towards the
cottage. This was her chance to accompany them on their
journey to the new village.

Jewels quickly hurried to grab the Corridor of
Hues she had hidden back underneath the seat of the
lounge chair. She kneeled to remove the book but struggled
with the strings that kept it in place.

Jewels heard someone behind her.

"Um, hello? Who are you?" Brooks approached Jewels from behind. "From the back, I can see you're not too bad looking."

Jewels kneeled back up and turned around to face her brother.

"Woah there!" Brooks jaw dropped to the floor. "Jewels? Is that you?"

"Yes, it's me! How do you like it, my dear brother?" Jewels twirled around in a small spin.

Brooks stared at her for a while and broke out in laughter.

"What is so funny? I want to laugh too!" Jewels said.

"Oh my gosh! I thought for sure you were a trollop!" Brooks laughed so hard his belly was hurting.

"Excuse me?" Jewels said.

Brooks stopped laughing. "What happened? I thought you loved it here and wanted to fit in."

"I was wrong!" Jewels said. "You guys were absolutely right. I'm not like them here. I want to go with you and Manny to the new village."

Brooks stood there, dazed by his sister's transformation and speechless by her confession.

Just then, Manny burst through the front door and tripped on his own feet. He fell straight down to the floor. Out of breath, he looked directly at Brooks and shouted, "They are coming for us! We must go now! Find Jewels so we can ask her to come. Hurry!"

Manny tried to regain his breath as he rose from the floor, he then looked at the strange woman on the other side of the room. "Jewels?"

"Yup! That's her," Brooks chuckled.

"Oh…my…heavens!" Manny fell back to the floor.

"No time to explain right now!" Jewels hurried over to help him up. "We must leave before they arrive. Take what you can, but only a few things."

"You're coming with us?" Manny nearly fell back on the floor again.

"Yes!" Jewels tried to release the Corridor of Hues from its bondage from under the lounge chair. It eventually gave way and the strings released the book from its hold.

She quickly put the book in her tote and cut two small holes between each side of the bag. She slid a thin rope through the holes and tied the tote around her waist.

"Let's hurry!" Jewels yelled. "Grab a few slices of bread for our journey, and a jug of water. We must go!"

Manny looked at Brooks. "What is going on?"

"I have no idea what's gotten into her," Brooks said. "I'm just as surprised as you are. Go now! Grab what you can like she said. We don't have much time before they get here!"

Brooks and Manny rushed to grab some food for their journey.

Meanwhile, Jewels climbed up the staircase that led to the roof deck of the cottage to view the village one last time. The memories poured through her mind. "I'm freeing myself and my brothers from this place!"

She took one last farewell gaze and noticed the villagers coming toward her cottage. They were carrying torches and stones in their hands. No longer did they look like the hardworking, conservative people that she once knew. They looked like a pack of starved hyenas ready to rip her family apart.

"He lied!" Jewels whispered to herself. "Mayor Pipers lied about the villagers wanting us to leave! They'd rather us be stoned!"

The three-siblings rushed out the door just barely escaping. While Mayor Pipers, who led the angry mob behind him, went inside the cottage but found no signs of the siblings anywhere. Mayor Pipers felt his blood boiling.

"Where have they gone?" someone shouted within the mob.

"They obviously have left this place," Mayor Pipers said, "and they were right on time!"

"Where could they have escaped to?" another one cried from within the crowd.

"It doesn't matter!" Mayor Pipers turned his face away from them. "Go, now! The traitors have left us. What happens to them will be much worse than anything we could have ever done."

* * * * *

Faster and faster the three siblings ran into the forest. Manny kept falling behind and could not keep up with Jewels and Brooks.

"Manny, get a move on!" Jewels shouted at him.

"I'm trying to keep up! I haven't run this fast in a while!" Manny yelled.

"Or ever!" Brooks chuckled.

After a while, they became very tired and stopped. They searched around and realized the mob was nowhere in sight.

"I think they're gone." Manny caught his breath as he fell to the ground. "I never thought I would see the day my legs would move that fast!"

"I hear ya!" Brooks huffed and puffed, taking deep breaths. "This whole thing is crazy!"

Jewels remained quiet, looking around the trees for the mob.

"You know what else is crazy? Our sister's brand-new makeover and rebel attitude. What universe am I living in?" Manny said.

Jewels turned and looked at her brothers, first Manny and then Brooks. Then cried, putting her hands over her face.

"They were going to stone us!" Jewels said. "He lied and told me they just wanted us to be removed."

"No surprise to me!" Manny lifted himself off the ground and leaned his body against a nearby tree. "Old man Pipers has always been up to no good!"

"Yup!" Brooks said. "He's nothing but a cold-blooded snake!"

Jewels grabbed both of her brothers and hugged them tightly. The two lads were surprised at this. Their sister had never hugged them like this before. Many times, she could barely make eye contact with them.

The village called the three siblings a "dysfunctional bunch." They didn't have a healthy relationship like the other families in the village. They were the only family that would argue endlessly at each other. It seemed this was how they expressed their love for one another, not knowing any other way.

"I've always admired you guys! I'm glad my eyes have been opened to the truth!" Jewels cried and hugged her brothers even tighter.

Manny and Brooks looked at each other and smiled, hugging their sister.

"I don't know what happened Jewels, but I'm so pleased you've finally come around!" Brooks hugged her tightly.

Manny smiled. "You've always been one of us."

The three hugged a few moments more and then ate some of the bread and drank from the jug they had brought for their journey, then continued their voyage to paradise.

* * * * *

They traveled for many hours and were exhausted from the long journey to the colorful village. Jewels grew tired of the journey and the same trees one after another.

"Are we almost there yet, you guys?" Jewels asked.

"I think so." Manny looked at the different pathways of the forest.

Jewels stopped dead in her tracks. "You think so? You don't remember where this place is?"

"We only saw this place once, and that was the day we told you about it," Brooks said.

Jewels came across a large oak tree and sat down beside it, with the Corridor of Hues still strapped tightly around her waist. She was tired of the journey and wanted to rest.

"So, all this time we've been walking, and no one remembers how to get there?" Jewels said.

"I think it's this way!" Manny pointed in the direction of the trees. "The trees near that path have dark hanging leaves."

Jewels looked in the direction to where Manny pointed, then looked back at him. "That's how you remember? All these trees have dark hanging leaves. Oh, for goodness sake. We're never getting out of here!"

Jewels put her hands on her face and shook her head.

"Calm down, Jewels! Brooks scanned the trails in the forest. "It will come to us and we will figure this out."

Jewels took the opportunity to get a few moments of rest, while her brothers talked amongst themselves to try and remember which route to take. She felt comforted by the large oak trees around her, like colossal towers, and she closed her eyes.

The forest was peaceful and calming but did not resemble anything near the stunning forest she saw within the Corridor of Hues. She fantasized about the colorful paradise but was interrupted by a noise in the forest.

"Vaara! Vaara!" the voice chanted.

What in the world?

Jewels saw her brothers not too far away, but they were not the ones making the sound.

"Vaara! Vaara!" the voice said.

Terrified, Jewels stood up and searched around the tree but tripped her foot against one of its large roots, hitting her head on the ground. She tried to pick herself up from the floor, but heard the voice echoing closer.

Jewels screamed as loud as she could.

Manny and Brooks ran back towards her. When they arrived, Jewels shook with fear and bled from a small head wound.

"What is going on, Jewels?" Manny asked.

"There's something here!" Jewels wiped the blood away from her head.

Brooks stared at her wound. "What's here?"

"I heard a voice in the forest," Jewels looked around.

"Well, I don't hear anything!" Manny walked around the oak tree.

"I don't either!" Brooks searched around with Manny.

"I want to get out of here!" Jewels tore some cloth from her dress and flattened it against her head. "Did you guys ever figure out where to go?"

"Yes, we figured it out," Brooks pointed to one of the routes.

"Great, let's go!" Jewels hurried her brothers.

* * * * *

As they continued their journey to the village, Jewels thought about the voice from earlier. Where did it come from? Hopefully it will show up again. This time she would find out what that thing is!

Not long after they had traveled further into the forest, the voice appeared once again.

"Vaara! Vaara!" the voice cried.

"Do you hear it now?" Jewels asked.

"Yes!" Brooks said. "I definitely hear it now!"

"Me too!" Manny ran up the path.

He stopped.

"Help me, you guys!" Manny caught his leg in a deep ditch.

Jewels and Brooks ran over to the trench where Manny's leg was trapped. They both lifted his leg out and rolled up his pant leg. It was badly bruised.

"It felt like something was pulling me down!" Manny said.

Jewels and Brooks looked at Manny's injury, which looked like a large handprint on his skin. However, this hand was unusual and looked nothing like a hand of a human, but appeared like curved, twisted roots tangled around his leg.

"Let's go back!" Jewels said.

"Go back to where?" Brooks said. "We cannot go back to our village! Don't you remember? They want us all dead!"

Jewels eyes were locked on Manny's leg. "It seems we all would be better off stoned than where we're going"

"No!" Manny tried to stand on his injured leg. "Look, everyone needs to relax. I'm fine! I have no idea what that was, or even if it was something in the ditch. Let's not lose sight of our mission!"

They then decided to rest for a while, so Manny could recover from his wound. After an hour or so, they walked back to the path, and the road was getting thinner and approaching a fork. There were many paths to take, and they were unsure which one was correct.

"I don't remember what path to take. Do you remember, Manny?" Brooks said.

"Nope. I've forgotten, too," Manny said.

"Excuse me?" Jewels looked at her brothers. "You guys told me earlier you knew where to go!"

"Not from here. That was weeks ago and we've since forgotten," Brooks said.

They were on a wild goose chase to a place Jewels now believed to be cursed. She didn't know if this place was worth it to continue between the mysterious voice in the forest, and Manny's surprising accident.

Things were getting stranger every passing moment, but then she saw the trees and sky slowly changing into brighter colors. The once cloudless pale, gray sky was being replaced with a bubbly shade of aqua blue.

The dark tree leaves were changing to different colors of green, which fell and carpeted the ground of the forest. Her attention then fell upon the rich, colored flowers that bloomed from the purple branches of the shrubs, swaying in the warm breeze.

"This must be the border of the forest!" Jewels watched their surroundings in wonder. "We are leaving the boundaries of our old village!"

They arrived at the fork of the pathway, and soaring through the sky, appeared a large bird. The sight of the creature was glorious. The fowl was of great size, a giant seven-foot beast. It looked like an enormous Rosella, with striking, piercing eyes, and a long narrow beak.

His feathers made Jewels' breath stop with their beauty, a mist of radiant colors that glowed like sunlight through the heavens. They gleamed red, orange, yellow, green, blue, indigo and violet, a splendid rainbow playing a colorful melody upon his body.

The bird glided above the earth in high, wide circles with its long, broad wings. The bird seemed to be scanning the ground below him. He then caught sight of the three-siblings and glared at them from afar. He dived down to a nearby tree where his large claws, shaped rather like hooks, grasped one of the branches. Then he peered down at them with a long gaze.

Jewels watched her brothers. They looked scared as if they believed the giant, feathered creature would devour them as his prey. But not Jewels. She marveled at the magnificent beast and bravely approached him, while her brothers carefully followed behind her. When she had gotten closer to the fowl, she didn't feel threatened, and the creature was peaceful towards them.

"Vaara! Vaara!" the bird chanted.

They now knew where the mysterious voice had come from.

"I think it wants us to follow him!" Jewels said. "It must be a part of the village within the Corridor of Hues. It's here to help us!"

"Great!" Manny and Brooks said.

"He needs a name!" Manny said.

Jewels thought about it for a moment. "Let's call him Seguimi!"

"Segga? What?" Manny asked.

"Seh-gee-mee," Jewels said.

"What does it mean?" Brooks said.

"It means follow me." Jewels smiled.

"Not bad!" Manny said.

The beast then lifted its great wings and flew slowly, leading them to the village within the pages of the Corridor of Hues.

CHAPTER FOUR

Meeting A Nightmare

THE SIBLINGS WERE starving as they followed Seguimi to their new home. The few pieces of bread and jug of water they had brought were long gone.

"I'm so tired and hungry." Manny took small steps to ease the pain of his leg.

"Me too," Brooks said. "I hope this bird is taking us to where some food is soon."

Jewels stayed silent as she watched Seguimi. His great wings flapped slowly above the earth as they followed behind him. Jewels noticed how the brighter hues transformed the forest almost completely.

The branching pathways of the forest, which before had caused confusion, now came together into their trail, creating one great road. The siblings saw that they were just moments away from entering the colorful village.

"I see the village now, you guys!" Jewels pointed in the new village's direction. "It's not too far ahead!"

Suddenly, walking along the pathway traveling through the forest, and now emerging into the village, an odd smell filled their noses. The smell made Jewels nauseous and she looked to see what direction the smell could be coming from, but only saw the great trees that surrounded them.

Manny limped along. "There's that strange smell again. It smells like it's coming from somewhere in the trees."

Just then, a bizarre creature with a long, skinny snout approached Jewels. It looked like a large rodent, and glowed both orange and green, the bright green of its body giving an unpleasant view inside its round stomach. The animal scurried around her feet swiftly, and in a blink of an eye, grabbed the Corridor of Hues from her waist.

It ran with the book into a hidden section of the forest that drifted off the pathway. Jewels ran behind the critter to save her book. She saw the creature from a distance climbing up a tree that was secretly hidden behind many other trees.

When the creature climbed the tree, it dropped the book then vanished from sight. She quickly ran to where the tree was and grabbed the Corridor of Hues from off the ground, and then strapped it firmly against her waist.

She took a moment to look over the tree that the creature had led her to. Fruit glowed from its branches. More trees with the same type of fruit surrounded her. Jewels went over to the tree and shook it. The tiny fruit rolled down to the floor.

She grabbed some from off the ground, looking at them strangely. They were small, oddly shaped, and soft.

What peculiar looking fruit.

Jewels put her nose to the fruit and the stench was awful. She saw that something appeared to be moving inside it.

"It's probably just some insect." Jewels felt starved, and neither the smell, nor a worm or two, was going to get in the way of her hunger.

When she sank her teeth into the fruit, a gush of sweet nectar erupted inside her mouth. The taste was heavenly. She had never tasted fruit this good. She quickly ate a few more.

Jewels put one in the pocket of her dress. Through the fabric, she felt the fruits squirm. She figured that's just how the fruit was there, inside the magical place, not paying it another mind.

She grabbed as many as she could and hurried back to find her brothers. She spotted them, far up the trail. Her brothers were too distracted by the enchanted forest and creatures that surrounded them and hadn't even noticed she was missing. She caught up with them and showed them the strange fruit.

"Holy Moly! Some food!" Manny ate two in one gulp.

Brooks stared at the mysterious fruit, squinting his eyes. "Why is the fruit moving?"

Jewels watched the fruit jiggle in his hands. "I think there's probably a worm in there or something."

"I don't know what's in there and I don't care!" Manny scarfed down another one. "All I know is that I'm hungry and these things taste amazing!"

Comforted by his sibling's delight for the fruit, Brooks ate them alongside his brother.

* * * * *

They walked throughout the pathways of the village, and Jewels noticed the strange creatures were every bright shade imaginable. They had various numbers of heads, two or more, which were either placed up right on their necks or sunk down into their chests. Those that did not have heads had eyes and mouths placed along their spines and rear ends.

When they finally arrived at the village, Jewels stood still, admiring its gorgeous, delightful display. The flamboyant colors of the village had a charming, bright attraction, and its beauty took her breath away. Jewels smiled, knowing she was finally home to her glorious paradise.

"It does truly exist!" Jewels smiled.

Seguimi flew down from the aqua blue sky and sat still on a lovely pink branch of a large tree, and the ripe green leaves shaded his gigantic body. He watched them with curiosity while they roamed the colorful dreamland.

Jewels caught a glimpse of the fowl from afar and gazed into his beautiful eyes. Seguimi looked at her, then flapped his wings and took flight.

"Thank you Seguimi, for all your help!" Jewels waived goodbye as the beast drifted far above the sky.

* * * * *

The three walked around the village to get acquainted with their new home, but just as her brothers had said before, there was no one there. Though, heaps of cottages surrounded them, they all wondered if anyone was inside.

They opened the doors of the cottages and searched them, hoping to find someone who lived there. Yet, despite all their efforts, there was no one in sight.

Walking along the village, they came upon a small well. The siblings were very thirsty and took turns drinking from it. It was the purest, most refreshing, crystal clear water they had ever tasted. Strangely, when they took a drink of the water, it mysteriously turned into a mystic red color.

Suddenly, something jumped out from behind them, scaring them all half to death. They turned around and saw that it was a dreadful-looking creature. They had never seen such an unusual being before. He mimicked an appearance of a mythical, horrifying gnome from someone's nightmare!

Jewels and her brothers had learned of gnomes from old folktales within their village. However, this gnome was the most hideous monster they could have ever imagined.

He had long, lanky arms like an octopus with scaly, bark-like skin, and his hands and arms looked like braided roots of a tree. His head slowly shifted from side to side, not quite touching his shoulder blades.

He wore a cap that fitted tightly around his skull, and his face was long and pointy. He had a wide grin that made him seem rotten to the core. His eyes were large and colorful, and mirrored the appearance of colored glass windows. He had no eyelids and could not blink.

He could only stare.

"Say there!" The ugly eyesore danced a little jig around them. "What brings you folks to my village?"

The siblings looked at each other horrified and said nothing.

When the monstrosity had finished dancing, his gaze settled upon Jewels who quickly caught his attention. He went over to her and smelled her dress from top to bottom.

Jewels had no idea what he was doing. She watched him with chills running down her spine.

A hare bolted across the grass nearby, and the gnome turned to pay attention to it. The gnome ran away from Jewels and blew directly on the small animal. The gnome's breath was a puff of shimmering colors that made the hare shake, and after a while it stopped and fell to the ground.

They were all speechless.

Jewels believed this gnome to be dangerous and whispered to her brothers to be careful with their words and to be silent.

The gnome picked up the hare and placed it in one of his large pants pockets and walked back over to the siblings. "So, I say again. What brings you folks here?"

"We have left our village," Jewels said, "and journeyed for a long time hoping that we could be a part of yours."

The gnome said nothing. His head flapped from side to side, his big smile spread across his long, pointy face—teasing them.

Then he laughed.

"You want to be a part of my village? Surely, you don't think it's that easy?" The gnome's strange voice echoed around them, as he rolled crazily around on the ground." I would like to get to know you a little better. Maybe even show you around a bit? You never know; you may change your mind."

"We would love to see more of this place," Manny said.

The gnome rose from the floor looking at the book that hung from Jewels' waist. "What is that tied around you, my dear?"

"It's my book. We call it the Corridor of Hues," Jewels said.

"I have many of those here." The gnome snatched the book from her waist.

The siblings looked at him in amazement as his long tree-root fingers turned through the pages of the book with such speed.

"This book is mines, not yours!" the gnome said.

Jewels looked at the creature. Her heart pounded. No one was certain how the Corridor of Hues entered the village. That had always been a mystery.

Jewels looked at the gnome, thinking of a way to explain. "These books for centuries have trickled their way into our village and—"

"I gave them to your village." The gnome gave the book back to her. "The paintings in this book are of my village, but they are still my books!"

Jewels had, until now, no idea that the gnome was the legendary culprit of the Corridor of Hues.

The gnome looked at Manny and Brooks. He walked towards them and stared. "You two chaps look very familiar. Haven't you've been here before?"

"No!" Manny said. "We've never been to this place."

"Are you sure?" the gnome said.

"Yes!" Brooks said. "This is our first time here."

"Aren't you three tired from your journey?" The gnome yawned, growing bored of them. "Would you like me to show you around now?"

"Yes, please," Jewels said.

"We would love to see the rest of the village," Manny said. "But we are so hungry. We haven't eaten much since we've left, just a few pieces of bread and some fruits close here to the village.

"Fruit around my village?" The gnome stared so hard at Manny. "Fruit does not grow on these trees."

"Are you the only one here?" Jewels tried to change the subject.

"No, my family is sleeping." The gnome led them on the pathway towards his cottage.

* * * * *

Jewels could not get over the beautiful collection of colors as they followed the gnome to his home. It was truly a magical place, just like stepping inside the Corridor of Hues. She was hopeful to be a part of such a wonderful paradise, even if it was the home of a monstrous gnome.

His family is sleeping, yet the only person that I see in the village is him! Where is everyone else?

Though many questions haunted Jewels, she was too distracted by the lovely colors that surrounded her and soon forgot about her doubts. She basked in the glorious place she wished to call her home, still holding the Corridor of Hues firmly in her hand.

The sky still had not fallen dark yet, and this fed Jewels' curiosity. "In our village, the sky is gloomy and gray in the day, but by this time it would have turned black."

"We don't have a nightfall here. It's always the light hours of the day," the gnome said.

The gnome turned to look back at Manny, pacing slowly behind them. "You're walking pretty stale there! What's wrong with your leg, pal?"

"I had an accident on the way here." Manny tried to pick up his pace.

"Oh, well that's too bad." The gnome grinned as if he were hiding an awful little secret. "These things do happen."

CHAPTER FIVE

A Supper of Horrors

THEY SOON ARRIVED at the gnome's handsome villa near the end of the village's path. The gnome approached his friendly cottage. "Here we are, gang!"

The gnome opened the bronze door and then stood in the doorway, staring at them. This time his stare was not the typical stare. This stare was growing longer, the colors in his eyes sparkling brighter, his smile becoming even wider and frightening, dancing across his pointy face.

"This is my humble abode. Come in and I will cook supper." The gnome's head swayed around like a doll's head not sewn on properly. "Does stew and tots sound like a good deal for dinner?"

The three agreed to his offer and walked through the main entrance.

* * * * *

The home was a beautifully decorated slice of heaven, and every room was bathed in bright sun-drenched colors. The eye-watering hues gleamed from every corner of the place.

Remarkable galleries, with exquisite oil canvases, shone from every space of the walls. Jewels admired his talent and believed him to be an exceptionally gifted artist. Many of his classical portraits showed the portrayal of a unique gathering of trees. Of all the paintings, those were the greatest work of his artistry.

"These trees inspire your passion," Jewels said.

"That's my family," the gnome said.

Jewels was not clear what he meant and continued to follow the gnome, behind her brothers. She noticed the many collections of books on each shelf. She was eager to see the elegant, beauty inside them. She placed her book on one of the shelves, and quickly grabbed one of the other books and opened it.

A puff of red raspberry-like goo splattered on her face from out of the book. The residue drip to the floor.

"You shouldn't touch things without asking." The gnome reached for a nearby cloth to wipe off Jewels face with.

Manny and Brooks broke out in laughter, looking at their sister's face. The gnome looked at the two brothers, and immediately they stopped laughing at her.

* * * * *

The gnome led them into a room in the back of the cottage. The room was full of colorfully upholstered antique furniture. The curtains were mint green, and the peach cream walls complemented the lavender ceilings. There was a breakfast nook, hand-decorated in bright floral patterns in the center of the room, and a leather-crafted wing chair placed at the head of the table.

"Please sit. I will go now to make supper." The gnome quickly left from them.

"Watching his head gives me motion sickness." Brooks whispered.

"Same here!" Manny said. "He needs to strap that thing on a bit tighter, so it can stay in one place!"

"Quiet!" Jewels whispered to them. "Have you two lost the rest of your minds? You saw what that thing is capable of, so try to keep your mouths shut!"

Reminded of the gnome's deadly magical power and what had happened to the hare, the two brothers became uneasy.

"He knows who we are. When we were here the first time, he must have seen us!" Manny said.

"You said you saw no one." Jewels watched the door for the gnome to return.

"We didn't, but he must have seen us here somewhere along the way," Brooks said.

They all agreed to say nothing else, for fear of being heard by the gnome.

After some time, the gnome returned with a bright mango colored stew and a basket of turquoise-colored sweet rolls. He placed the food on the table, and Jewels heard his twig-like fingers crunching and snapping against the dishware. He poured himself and each one of them a tall glass of water from a lime-green jug, then placed it on the table alongside the basket of rolls.

The supper's smell was delightful, and the meal was nothing like they had ever tasted before. It was just delicious!

The gnome stared at Manny and Brooks as he took a seat in his wing chair, facing them at the table. The two brothers ate like animals, as fast as they could, smacking their lips with food running down their faces.

"Don't forget to chew your food!" the gnome said. "You want to be able to enjoy your last meal."

Brooks almost choked on his food. "Our last meal?"

"What do you call your kind?" the gnome said. "I always tend to forget."

"We're called humans." Jewels took another bite of the brightly hued rolls. She noticed the sweet rolls had turned she and her brothers' tongues into very bright shades.

The gnome shifted his attention to Jewels for a few moments then fixed his gaze back on Manny and Brooks. He stared at the two in silence. Every movement they made his colorful eyeballs followed.

"You know, it's funny that you two said you've never been here before," the gnome said.

Terrified of the gnome, the brothers remained silent and kept their eyes on the table. Jewels watched the gnome studying her brothers with his eyes.

"I didn't realize that book was yours," Jewels said.

"Every century or so I give your village my books," the gnome said. "I enjoy giving your species a chance to see a marvelous world beyond theirs. However, this never works out as well as planned, and motivates many of your troublemakers to journey here to my village.

"Many of these books have in our village have been destroyed," Jewels said. "This is probably the last one left."

"Oh, how perfectly lovely!" the gnome said. "I share my precious artwork with your kind, and it gets ruined. Well, isn't that just wonderful?"

The gnome was becoming annoyed, and Jewels watched his head sway faster, now pressing against his shoulder blades.

The gnome looked at them. "It appears that only the worse of your village comes to see me. Your good-for-nothing lawbreakers just love to bring themselves here, and this is upsetting!"

"You know what else is funny?" The gnome laughed, which made his head jog around his neck. "For centuries, you humans, have infested my village. You all drank from my well earlier, polluting it with your filthy mouths and hands!"

The gnome looked upon his lovely paintings that hung majestically on the walls. Then he looked directly over at Manny and Brooks. "Trying to explain to a blind man that there is a world beyond his shadows is almost next to impossible! You humans love to make your way over here to give me such grief! I wonder if the only answer to my troubles is to destroy your village?"

When the brothers heard the gnome say these things, they grew even more afraid, and the room was silent.

"I apologize for myself and my brothers for drinking from your well," Jewels said. "The journey here was tiring, and we were very thirsty. My brothers and I admire your village greatly and have journeyed here at all costs."

"Because you are criminals and you had no choice!" the gnome yelled.

"Yes, we are outcasts of our village," Jewels said. "However, I have treasured your village from the time I was a young child. I have kept the book for many years, and I've cherished it since the first day I discovered it."

Jewels looked around for her book and realized it was not with her. She had left it on the shelf with the other books of the gnome's collection.

"Is that right?" the gnome said. "I did see that you had taken good care of it."

"Yes," Jewels said. "That's why it has never been destroyed, even when I was commanded to do so. This is a beautiful world that my brothers and I desperately want to be a part of. We were cast out because we are not like the people in our village, nothing more."

"Sounds like me!" the gnome said. "I believe you three and myself are one in the same."

"What do you mean?" Jewels asked.

"Frankly, I can relate to your experience," the gnome said. "I rarely sleep. It makes me weak when I awaken and takes me days to recover. Unlike your kind, who recover quickly from their rest."

"You said your family sleeps?" Jewels said.

"Yes, they love it!" the gnome said. "I'm nothing like them. I feel that I'm more useful when I can be awake to work on my crafts. Sleep weakens my kind, and rarely do they come about."

The gnome turned his attention back to Manny and Brooks. "They're unusually quiet. When they came here before, they disturbed my family and I during our rest. The rarest of times when I slept, these two came into my village. I spotted them before they had left, but I was too weak to catch up to them. Now, I will ask you two again. Weren't you here before?"

Manny and Brooks kept their heads down and said nothing.

"Speak now!" the gnome banged his head on the table.

"Yes, we lied," Manny said. "We have come here before!"

"I apologize for my brother's actions," Jewels said. "They certainly could not have known you and your family were at rest."

"Don't worry about it," the gnome said. "Like I said, this has been happening to me for a very long time."

"Where do you and your family sleep?" Jewels said.

For a moment the gnome ignored her to stare at Manny and Brooks. He looked directly at them, his head touching the opposite side of his shoulder blades.

"We sleep in trees." The gnome turned to Jewels. "We are not humans like you, your brothers, and the ones from the village you have left. We don't sleep in beds and rarely do we sit on chairs."

The gnome sipped the water from his glass. "I've had human visitors entering my village for centuries, yet still, I enjoy getting acquainted with my company during their last meal."

They all turned and looked at each other when the gnome mentioned the supper being their last, again.

"Why do you say this supper is our last?" Jewels said. "You have already done this twice now."

The gnome said nothing. His disturbing gaze left the brothers to look upon Jewels.

"Since I met you, my dear," the gnome said, "I have smelled a charming scent that stains your dress. It smells very familiar to me. I thought it would be rude of me to ask when I smelled you earlier. I felt we had not yet been fully acquainted, but now I must know! What makes your clothing reek of that splendid odor?"

The gnome's head weaved in excitement.

Jewels did not know what odor he was speaking of. She had never worn perfume or any other fragrance that could have sparked the gnome's interest.

She thought about it for a moment and realized it was the fruit they had eaten earlier. Jewels remembered she had placed one in the pocket of her dress. She took the fruit out of her pocket and placed it on the table. She noticed it no longer moved.

"The smell is coming from this fruit," Jewels said. "My brothers and I ate many of these earlier in the forest near your village. We were so hungry. You said fruit does not grow on your trees, but I did find these growing there."

The gnome stared at the fruit in silence. His smile was suddenly replaced by a long, hideous frown painted across his face. His head for the first time locked down, into one place. The gnome stood up, out of his chair and went to where Jewels had laid the fruit.

He picked it up and wept.

The siblings watched the gnome weep and tears from every shade of color fell from his large eyes. They didn't understand why the gnome wept over a simple piece of fruit.

"What's wrong?" Jewels asked. "It was only a piece of fruit. There is more in the outskirts of the village."

"As I said before," the gnome said, "no fruit grows on these trees. These are my family, and they were sleeping."

CHAPTER SIX

It's Coming

THERE WAS A long pause as they all froze in horror. Jewels knew now why the fruits were moving, because they weren't fruit. They were his family! The three were horrified and none could find the words. Jewels and her brothers had no idea what was going to happen, while they watched the gnome sob for his loved ones.

Suddenly, the gnome's weeping stopped.

They looked at the floor where he had cried and saw that his tears made a puddle of gold-streaked water that covered the floor.

The gnome turned suddenly at them. In the blink of an eye he jumped on top of the table, causing a great impact as they all fell back in their chairs, hitting the ground.

His large eyes turned every color possible then stopped at stone-cold black. His arms, already long and wavy, stretched longer, like branches from a tree, and his head tossed violently around his body. He spun around a few times then ran from the cottage.

They hurried to help one another up and looked out the windows, trying to find where he was.

"You think he's coming back?" Brooks said.

"Maybe you should go out there and ask him!" Manny said.

"Quiet, you two!" Jewels searched out the window to see where the monster had gone.

"What should we do?" Manny said.

"Shh!" Jewels said.

"I don't see him anywhere in clear sight. We must leave now!" Jewels yelled.

Jewels and her brothers ran out of the gnome's home.

"Oh no! I forgot to get my book!" Jewels looked back at the cottage.

"Leave it! Let him have his book!" Brooks shouted.

* * * * *

They ran as fast as they could back into the colorful forest and the gnome was close on their tail. His legs moved at an incredible speed, as his tree root feet and hands grew larger and longer, sinking down into the earth.

They were terrified and ran even faster.

Manny was still in pain from his leg. He trailed behind. Jewels and Brooks, noticing he needed help, ran back towards him.

"No guys keep going!" Manny shouted. "I'll catch up with you two soon. Don't worry!"

Jewels was saddened that her brother had turned them away but honored his wishes, running as fast as she possibly could. After a while, she stopped to catch her breath, noticing her and Brooks were deeper into the forest.

She did not see the gnome or Manny anywhere in sight.

Jewels searched with Brooks to see how far Manny had trailed behind, walking further down the pathway and still did not find him. They turned back, went over every step from the last time they saw Manny, but he was nowhere.

"How could you guys bring me to a place like this?" Jewels asked.

"We didn't know he knew who we were. We had never seen this creature before," Brooks said.

The lovely village of colors that she had dreamt about from within the Corridor of Hues was now a terrifying nightmare, and she was unable to awaken from it.

"Look at what we've done!" Jewels cried and fell to her knees. "Our brother is missing because of this disaster, most likely at the mercy of that monster. What's worse is that we ate his family and he is seeking his revenge. Not only have we put ourselves in grave danger but our village as well!"

"Our village? You mean the village where they wanted us stoned? I'm not ever going back there!" Brooks walked away, searching for Manny.

"We have to warn them that he is to come!" Jewels followed behind him.

"I'm going back to find our brother," Brooks said.

"I'm going with you!" Jewels cried.

"No, Jewels!" Brooks yelled. "It doesn't take both of us."

"I'm not leaving you like we did Manny." Jewels cried and grabbed Brooks. "You're all I have left!"

Brooks pushed her away from him and tears filled into his eyes. "Manny is still around! Don't ever say something like that to me again. I'm going to head back to find him. You need to go and warn the village or whatever you decide to do."

"We're going together. You're not leaving me!" Jewels screamed and grabbed Brooks again.

As Jewels struggled with Brooks, she noticed he was getting shorter by the second. A trench was forming around his feet, and his body sinking into the ground. In a flash, his knees were soon in the belly of the trench.

"Something is pulling me down!" Brooks dropped further into the ditch.

Jewels rushed to her brother's aide and with all her might grabbed him, forcing him upwards. Brooks used every ounce of his strength to release himself from bondage while she helped to pull him out. Their efforts somehow worked, and his legs slowly reappeared from the earth.

Without warning, a puff of sparkling dust arose from the ditch. The dust was so powerful that when Jewels inhaled it just for a brief second, it knocked her feet away to the ground. She could feel her body weakening from the toxins. She crawled away, holding her breath to carefully not breathe anymore of the fatal poison.

When she got far enough away to recover, she saw Brooks fighting with every fiber of his being to escape his imprisonment. The roots bounded his body and jerked him down towards the ground. He yelled for his sister, Jewels, but realized he no longer had the ability to speak, and the shimmering cloud of dust choked him.

Jewels watched in horror as her brother sank deeper into the ground. The dust filled the air all around him, and he shook nonstop while the roots climbed his chest. Then Brooks stopped moving. His body grew lifeless and fell backwards.

"Just like the hare." Jewels whispered to herself, tears falling from her eyes.

The roots moved to Brooks shoulders, neck, and finally covered his entire head, then forced his entire body down into the pits of the earth.

Jewels became lightheaded and passed out.

* * * * *

She was awoken by a loud voice coming from the trees. The voice sounded as if it was a crowd of people speaking all at once. She thought she was surrounded but looked around and saw no one.

"You and your village will bear the same fate!" the voice said.

Jewels had grown weaker from breathing the poisons that came out of the trench. She tried to raise herself up from off the ground but couldn't. She felt something crawling up her foot, then quickly to her ankles and then her knees. It felt heavy on her legs and squeezed them tightly.

She looked at what was causing the unbearable pain and to her terror it was the horrifying roots that had taken her brother. Jewels tried to shake the roots off her as much as she could, but she was too weak. She tried to crawl on her knees to try to escape but it grabbed her and pulled her down. A ditch formed around her frail body.

Slowly, Jewels sank into the ground. She cried knowing that this would be the end, but quickly remembered Seguimi, the beautiful bird of colors.

Where has he gone? Could he help?

She screamed with the little energy that she had left and shouted, "Vaara, Vaara!"

After a moment, she saw the bird had not come.

The roots climbed up her body, now beyond her waist. With all her might again, she hollered for the beast, "Vaara, Vaara!"

The bird still did not come.

Jewels sobbed even more as the roots moved to her chest and then to her shoulders. She closed her eyes as the horrifying things slowly wrapped around her neck, and then her head.

* * * * *

"Squawakkkk!" shrieked a loud noise.

Jewels felt her body lift, floating in the air. She opened her eyes and saw that it was, indeed, Seguimi. He had set her free from the bondage of the roots and they dropped from her body. He clutched her firmly in his large claws and whisked her away, soaring through the air high above.

Seguimi moved his wings at a great speed, as if something came after them. The earth below shook as if there were a great stampede throughout the forest. Jewels looked back and saw something moving fast through the trees and heard high-pitched voices screaming, which sent chills down her spine.

They soon passed the boundary of the forest, which led to the village where she and her brothers had been banished. The forest that was once of the wonderful bright colors turned back to the familiar dull shades she knew too well.

The high-pitched voices were now far in the distance, and Jewels looked up and saw Seguimi's stunning feathers turn a dark hue. His wings were no longer the bright, flamboyant colors that she admired so dearly. They were now as dark as those of a crow.

Seguimi's speed dropped at an alarming rate and he drifted lower to the earth. The majestic beast was in unbearable pain, but he wanted to save her.

Jewels was trying to understand what had caused his shocking transformation. Crossing into her village's border must have made him ill.

The bird was dying.

"Seguimi, let me go!" Jewels shouted. "You have done what you can. Let me down into the forest of my village!"

She didn't know if the bird understood what she said, but she tried to wriggle out of his huge claws and continued to scream for him to let her go. Seguimi felt her struggling to escape from his clutches, and he plunged down toward the ground, placing her safely on the earth.

The bird's pain clearly tormented him, as he became darker and weaker by the second.

Seguimi looked at Jewels as if he knew he would never see her again. Then with all his great might, he flew back across the border towards the village within the pages of the Corridor of Hues, and his colors reappeared.

* * * * *

Jewels saw that her village was not far away, and she was determined to warn them about the gnome who was to destroy them all. She crawled towards the village, but she was too weak to keep going.

Lying on the on the ground, she vomited.

What seemed like hours passed, and she could feel something approaching her, but she couldn't make out what it was, her eyesight was so blurred.

Two hunters of her village had spotted her from afar. Each held their weapon at the ready, believing she was a wounded animal within the forest. They came closer to Jewels.

"Who is this?" one of them said.

Jewels' hearing had left her and could not hear them speak, while they looked at her short dress and trimmed hair.

"This may be a trollop!" The hunter kneeled.

Jewels felt the hunter checking her pulse with his fingers on her neck, and then slowly opened her mouth. When the hunters caught view of her brightly colored tongue, they both jumped back far away from her.

"She has Locky disease!" The other hunter moved further away. "Leave her here!"

Jewels tried to bring herself to speak but could not. She had lost her ability to talk long before they had found her. The ground trembled as the creature moved closer toward her village. She shivered in pain until her body became still, and silently drifted away.